This book is dedicated to
Sean
xxx xx x

Down at the dump amid coils and springs
Surrounded by rubbish and unwanted things,

Sat an empty old box, battered and worn,
Dark smudgy marks and edges all torn.

No longer useful, long past his prime
Thoughts racing back to a happier time.

He'd carried a puppy on his way to the vets
He spent months as a home to a tangle of nets.

He carried the bunting to a small village fair,
And returned full of books with no room to spare.

He helped to move house, propped open a door,
Helped make some space on the nursery floor.

But now here he sat, with no part to play,
Longing to be used with each passing day.

A shout from the entrance, a man and his son
"We're building a go-kart, this will be fun!"

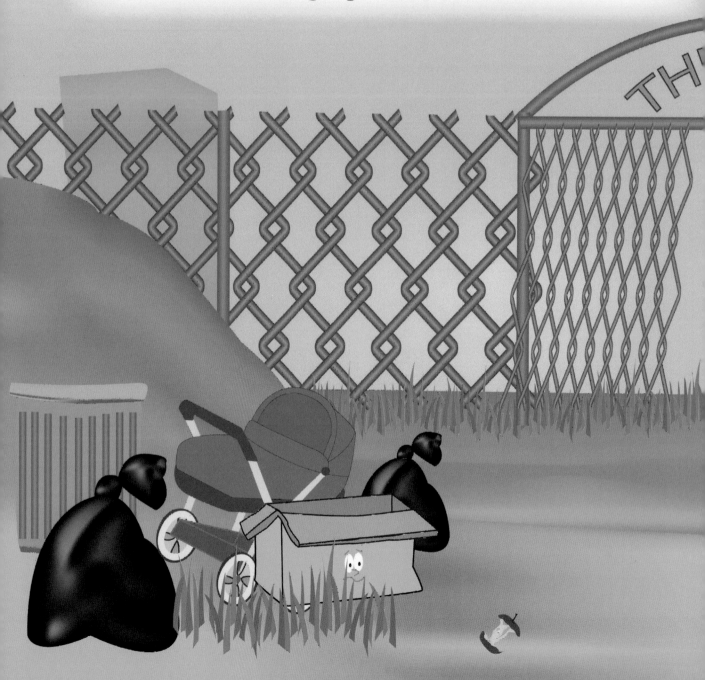

They'd made a long list of all that they'd need,
And jumping about, the boy started to read…

"Wheels and wood, some paint and some string
We'll make a go-kart fit for a king!"

Off they both went to sift through the scrap,
They found bicycles, kettles, a discarded cap.

Unwanted paintings, a stuffed elephant's trunk,
A whole host of treasures amidst rubble and junk.

It didn't take long to locate every part,
It was going to be a magnificent kart!

With pieces piled up they were ready for home,
But there was no way they could carry it all on their own.

The boy looked around scanning the rocks,
When his gaze fell upon our sad lonely box.

The box couldn't believe it, his dreams had come true,
He finally had something useful to do.

To the car they all headed, the box filled up high,
A smile on his face and a contented sigh.

The following day Dad and son made a start,
The pieces laid out to build the go-kart.

With each piece removed, in the doubts creep,
Once this is over, it's back to the heap.

The last item removed, empty once more,
The box sat discarded, alone on the floor.

Pushed to the side, his heart gave a squeeze
As he heard a small voice say, "Can I have this please?"

He was carried inside and placed on the ground,
In a room that was filled with treasures abound.

There were crayons and glue, empty bottles, a straw,
Scattered haphazardly over the floor.

The boy grabbed the box, a smile on his face
"Today you're a rocket, let's go into space!"

There was gluing and sticking as day turned to night,
But at last, he was ready to take his first flight.

His mission – to take his new friend to Mars,
"Whoosh!" they both cried as they zoomed through the stars.

Next day the adventure was out on the sea,
So, the boy set to work as quick as could be.

A sail and a mast, some bottles to float,
And a colourful flag completed the boat.

The mission – to find the lost hidden loot,
And avoid Captain Obi, a dangerous old brute.

Oh, the adventures they had, some near and some far,
A plane straight to Africa, then the seaside by car.

He was an ambulance, police car, a red fire truck,
And our little box couldn't believe his good luck.

He couldn't wait to see the next place to explore,
Just using the junk from the boy's bedroom floor.

The possibilities are endless, adventures are waiting,
So, unlock your imagination and go get creating!

Printed in Great Britain
by Amazon

69350334R00020